FLOTSAM
AND
JETSAM

Books by the same author

Waking Merlin

FLOTSAM AND JETSAM

Tanya Landman

illustrated by Ruth Rivers

WALKER BOOKS

First published 2006 by Walker Books Ltd
87 Vauxhall Walk, London SE11 5HJ

2 4 6 8 10 9 7 5 3 1

Text © 2006 Tanya Landman
Illustrations © 2006 Ruth Rivers

The right of Tanya Landman and Ruth Rivers to be identified as
author and illustrator respectively of this work has been asserted by
them in accordance with the Copyright, Designs and Patents Act 1988

This book has been typeset in StempelSchneidler

Printed and bound in Great Britain by Creative Print and Design
(Wales), Ebbw Vale

British Library Cataloguing in Publication Data:
a catalogue record for this book is available from the British Library

ISBN-13: 978-1-84428-119-0
ISBN-10: 1-84428-119-1

www.walkerbooks.co.uk

For Rod, who provided the inspiration;
and Isaac and Jack, who listened
T. L.

For Helen and Ben
R. R.

IN THE BEGINNING...

The timbers of a wooden rowing boat creaked as the waves lapped and slapped against it. The night was clear and cool with a moon so full and bright that it cast shadows of an old man and a young boy who sat together, fishing in friendly silence.

The sea was calm on the surface, but in its inky depths something stirred.

Quietly – so quietly that the man and boy didn't even turn their heads – a knotted tangle of driftwood and string broke the surface. Ripples

spread outwards. The tangle was gripped by the tide and carried slowly past the boat towards the distant cliffs.

The boy broke the silence. "What's that, Grandpa?"

The old man looked at the wave-worn wood and string. "It's just flotsam and jetsam," he replied.

The boy watched it drift away. For a moment, he thought he could see a face – no, two faces – peering up at the stars. But maybe it was just a trick of the moonlight. He shrugged, and went back to his fishing.

Two pairs of eyes blinked. They didn't know where they had come from or why or how, but now they knew their names.

"Flotsam and Jetsam," they whispered softly.

"That's who we is."

There was a long pause, and then one of them asked,

"But which is who?"

An even longer pause followed. Then the other answered. "Flotsam. That's who you is," she said firmly. "Jetsam. That's who I is." And Flotsam nodded in agreement.

They floated onwards, until at last the sea laid them gently on the soft sand of a tiny beach. The two small figures untangled themselves and stood up.

Jetsam's hair was wild and knotted old string. The top of Flotsam's bald head was worn as smooth and as round as a pebble. Both had jet-black eyes peering out from brown driftwood faces. Ropy legs ended in chunky, toeless feet. Stringy arms bore shapely hands, with nimble, stick-like fingers.

They looked at each other in wonder. Then, clasping one another tightly by the hand, they began to explore.

THE HOUSE ON THE BEACH

Twice a day the tide went out. Sea anemones drew in their sticky fingers. Limpets sucked down tight on rocks. Crabs scuttled to hide in pools as the water ebbed away. Twice a day the sea returned, flooding rock pools and cooling sun-baked sand. There was a magical moment of high water when the sea paused and seemed to rest for a minute before the tide turned. And it was then that it would lay down a line of strange and wonderful things on Flotsam and Jetsam's little beach.

11

The sea brought rubber rings and sun hats lost by small children on bigger beaches. It brought burger boxes and plastic bottles tossed by thoughtless holidaymakers over the sides of ferries. Wooden boxes that slid from cargo ships during heavy storms were washed up on the shore, as well as a brightly painted biscuit tin and a silver thimble that had rolled from the deck of a huge ocean liner. The sea dredged up mermaids' purses and cuttlefish bones from its depths. It plucked strange shells from

distant shores
– some that
were covered
in spikes,
some that
glowed like
jewels, and others that
were as smooth and shiny as mirrors.

All these things, the sea laid on the sand
for Flotsam and Jetsam to find.

The beach had been their home ever since
that moonlit night when something had
stirred in the inky depths of the sea, and
they had been drawn to the surface. And all
that time they had lived in a small cave at
the foot of the cliffs.

Their bed was a box which had the word JA FA painted on the side. They had lined it with dried seaweed and topped it with an old baby's blanket. Fishing floats, bits of netting and exotic shells hung from the ceiling above the bed. Their table was a biscuit tin, and their dining chairs were upturned drinks cans. There was only one armchair – a punctured football – in which Flotsam and Jetsam had to take turns.

Sometimes they squeezed
into it together, but that was
never comfortable for very long.

They had stuffed yoghurt pots with food:
dried seaweed was made into seaweed
crispies and tea. Flower heads of sea pinks
and sea campion harvested in the summer
were then turned into marmalades and
jellies. Sea lettuce and kelp were kept damp
in jam jars to make tasty pies, stews and

fritters. And all around the walls the treasures that Flotsam and Jetsam gathered from the beach were stacked high.

It was a nice cave, as caves go, but there were two big problems. Firstly, it was a little on the damp side. When it rained, the water would find its way through cracks in the cliffs and dribble down the moss on the walls. Jetsam complained that the damp made the cave smell funny. Secondly, they had no chimney. In the winter, when Flotsam lit a fire, smoke filled the cave making their eyes water and their throats sore.

One chilly winter's evening, a storm was brewing. The wind was mumbling, the sea was grumbling and the rain was lashing down.

As usual, the cave was full of smoke and the rainwater was oozing down the walls. As they stumbled around in the thick haze,

Flotsam stubbed his foot on an old piece of drainpipe. Jetsam tripped and sent a pile of empty yoghurt pots flying. They couldn't see to tidy up – they couldn't see to do anything. There was nothing for it but to go to bed early.

Flotsam and Jetsam huddled together in the JA FA bed and listened to the storm. It raged all through the night. The wind howled and the sea screamed, and then suddenly there was a loud *thump!* as if something heavy had been thrown onto the beach. Flotsam and Jetsam put their heads under the blanket, and waited for morning.

When the sun rose, the sea had calmed down. It was low tide. Flotsam climbed out of bed and peered at the sky from the mouth of the cave.

"Is it sunning?" called Jetsam from beneath the blanket.

"No."

"Is it raining?"

"No."

Jetsam threw the blanket aside and sat up. "Well, what is it doing?"

Flotsam looked at the grey sky. He held out a hand. "'Tis drizzling," he decided.

"Us must wear our Walkers, then," said Jetsam firmly.

They both pulled a crisp packet over their heads. These were very useful for keeping out the worst of the wet.

Then they set off to see what had *thumped* in the night.

It was the biggest thing the sea had ever brought them.

They had seen something like it once before: one had been floating on the sea on the moonlit night they had landed on their little beach.

Jetsam walked all around it once. Then she turned and walked all the way back again, and after a very long time, she said, "That's a boat, that is. Sure as waves is waves. Sure as barnacles is barnacles."

Flotsam nodded.

Jetsam carried on talking. "What can us *do* with it? 'Tis full of holes. 'Tis cracked down one side. It won't float. But it must be useful for something or the sea wouldn't have brought it to us, and that's the truth."

"Ah," said Flotsam, rubbing his nose.
"Well … maybe us could keep things in it."

Jetsam looked at him. "Maybe us could…
It would give us more room in the cave.
But us had better move it, or the sea will
take it back."

The tide had turned and was edging up
the beach.

They tried to move the boat. It was only
little – a child could have dragged it – but
Flotsam and Jetsam were very small, and
they couldn't shift it, no matter how hard
they tried. They pulled and they pushed
and they tugged and they heaved, but at last
they gave up, and sat on the sand panting.

"What shall us do?" asked Jetsam. "The sea
will take back our treasure, sure as prawns is
prawns. Sure as lobsters is lobsters."

But Flotsam cupped his bald head in his
stick-like fingers and said quietly, "I is
thinking."

Jetsam watched the sea creep closer and closer. It was very hard sitting still and saying nothing. By the time Flotsam spoke again, the sea was further up the beach and Jetsam was dancing from foot to foot and chewing the ends of her fingers in a worried way.

"I've thunk," said Flotsam. He stood up slowly and picked a large piece of driftwood off the sand. "Dig," he said. "That's what us needs to do."

He started to dig away the sand from the side of the boat that was furthest from the sea, making the ground flat and level.

Jetsam didn't understand what Flotsam was doing or why. But he had thunk a thought, and she knew it would be a good one. So she found another piece of driftwood and started scraping sand away from the other end.

And as they dug and scraped and shifted the sand, the sea inched up the beach, one wave at a time. It was almost touching the boat, reaching out wet fingers to claim it back, when Flotsam and Jetsam met in the middle. They had finished. The sand behind the boat was as smooth and as flat as the sea on a calm day.

Flotsam took the two pieces of driftwood and rammed them hard under the side of the boat nearest the sea so they stuck out like levers.

Jetsam looked at Flotsam. The sea was washing around their ankles.

"Right," said Flotsam with a slight wobble in his voice. "Now us needs to climb."

"Climb?" asked Jetsam worriedly. "But I is scared of heights."

Flotsam didn't hear her. He was already clambering up the side of the boat. Jetsam followed, eyes straight ahead as she tried

not to look down. Soon
they were both standing
on the edge of the boat.

"'Tis a terrible long way
down," squeaked Jetsam.
Her voice trailed away into
a small, scared whisper.
She swallowed hard.
"What does us do now?"

"Us jumps," said Flotsam.
He was nervous, but trying
hard not to let it show.

"Jumps?!" The word
wouldn't quite come out
and Jetsam made a little
gasping noise instead.

"Ready?"

Jetsam tried to say no,
but the word still wouldn't
come out.

"Steady?"

The word wouldn't budge. All that came out of Jetsam's mouth was a faint whimper.

"*GO!*" cried Flotsam with determination, taking Jetsam by the hand.

"*No!*" squeaked Jetsam.

But it was too late. Flotsam took an almighty leap high into the air, pulling Jetsam with him.

"*Eeeeeek!*"

Thump!

They crashed down onto the pieces of driftwood.

It worked a bit like a seesaw. When Flotsam and Jetsam landed on one end of the wood, the other end flipped the boat up onto its side. It hung there for a moment. Then it rolled over onto the flat sand that they had dug away. The boat lay upside down and out of the sea's reach, just beyond the highest high-water mark of the highest spring tide.

Flotsam and Jetsam picked themselves up and brushed the sand off each other.

"Ah," said Flotsam happily. "Just look at that. 'Tis lovely. 'Tis good that way up. Us can keep lots of things in there. 'Tis a very useful cupboard."

"Oh no it isn't," said Jetsam. She had recovered from the shock of flying and was taking charge again. "'Tisn't a cupboard. Oh no. 'Tis a *house*. A *proper* little house. 'Tis better than the cave. Sure as rocks is rocks. Sure as jellyfish is jellyfish."

And it was.

They filled the holes in the boat with treasures from the cave. Jam jars were turned into circular windows just like a ship's portholes. Smaller gaps were plugged with moss and seaweed. The old piece of drainpipe became a perfect chimney.

"Us can light a fire now and still see!" exclaimed Flotsam.

The big
crack in
the side
of the boat
became the
door. Flotsam
and Jetsam
covered the
floor with bits
of fishing net and
sacking to make a cosy carpet. Then they
dragged their JA FA bed across the beach
and pushed it inside. One by one they
brought the yoghurt pots of dried seaweed
and the jam jars of wet seaweed. They
rolled the biscuit-tin table, carried the
drinks-can chairs and pushed the football
armchair until at last all their furniture and
food was safely inside. And finally they
built a fireplace in the middle and ringed it
with pebbles.

"'Tis proper cosy," sighed Jetsam happily.
"'Tis proper marvellous. Us will like it here.
Sure as pinks is pinks. Sure as sunstars is
sunstars."

And then, feeling very happy, they sat
leaning against the side of their new house,
and listened to the sea as they watched the
sun sink slowly beneath the waves.

The old man and the young boy walked the cliff path every day. It led to a small harbour where a wooden fishing boat bobbed up and down, waiting for them like an eager puppy.

If they had paused for a moment and looked down from the cliffs, they would have seen a very tidy little beach with an upturned boat in the middle. If they had looked really hard, they might have noticed an old piece of drainpipe poking out of it. And if they'd watched on a cold day, they might have seen a whisper of smoke curling out of the drainpipe, as if a cosy fire was burning inside.

But they didn't look. They didn't even glance down. To them it was just a little beach, nestling at the bottom of high cliffs: impossible to get to on foot and not worth visiting by boat – too small to bother with.

But it was the whole world to Flotsam and Jetsam.

SEAGULL
TROUBLE

A strange sound woke Flotsam and Jetsam one morning. It wasn't the whoosh of the sea, or the roar of the wind, or the patter of rain. It was something quite new – a scratching on the roof of their boat house.

Flotsam and Jetsam looked at each other nervously.

"I don't like the sound of that," said Jetsam. "I don't like the sound of that at all. Something's up there. Sure as whelks is whelks. Sure as sea slugs is sea slugs."

They huddled under the blanket in their JA FA bed and listened. Heavy, scratchy footsteps plodded all the way along the roof. There was a short silence. Then the footsteps plodded all the way back again.

"'Tis a creature," said Jetsam. "A terrible big one." And they both turned pale as they imagined the large creature with scratchy claws that was making itself at home on the roof of their boat house.

"What shall us do?" worried Jetsam.

Flotsam cupped his bald head in his stick-like fingers and said quietly, "I is thinking." And after a long pause, in which the clawed feet walked the length of the roof and back one more time, he said, "I've thunk."

"Yes?" said Jetsam eagerly.

"I thinks us should have a cup of tea. If us waits long enough, the creature might go away."

Flotsam climbed out of the JA FA bed,

34

keeping an anxious eye on the ceiling. He fed the fire with lolly sticks and bits of driftwood, and put a tin can of water on to boil. As soon as it was hot, he dropped little black pieces of dried seaweed into the water. When it smelt good and salty, he poured it into two empty limpet shells and carried them over to Jetsam.

They sat in the JA FA bed and drank their tea, hoping that the sound – and whatever was making it – would go away.

But it didn't.

"Us will have to have a look," said Jetsam.

"Yes," agreed Flotsam. "Off you goes, then."

"I was thinking us might go together."

"Was you?" said Flotsam.

"Yes."

"Oh."

And then they both said nothing for a bit while they listened to the scratching.

"Us must ask it to stop," said Jetsam. "Whatever it is."

"Yes," agreed Flotsam.

"If us is nice and polite it might go away," added Jetsam hopefully.

"Hmm," said Flotsam, not sounding very sure.

They finished their tea, and looked at each other worriedly. Then they climbed out of the JA FA bed and peered out of their doorway.

"Us must make a dash for the cave," said Jetsam firmly. "Us will be safe there. Then us can see what's making that noise."

They clasped each other's hands tightly, and when Jetsam shrieked "NOW!!!" they sprinted across the beach as fast as their ropy little legs could carry them. And as they ran, they could hear a horrible cackling sound. Whatever the creature was, it seemed to be laughing at them.

When they reached the cave, breathless, panting and scared, they looked back at their boat house.

A black-backed gull – a very big, very mean-looking seagull – was standing on their roof. It was taller than Flotsam and Jetsam, and its sharp, pointy beak was as long as a razor shell.

It was a monster.

The bird looked at them with a nasty expression in its yellow eyes: a spiteful, bullying look. Flotsam and Jetsam shuddered.

"Go and talk to it," urged Jetsam, nudging Flotsam in the ribs. "Go on. You is braver than me."

"I doesn't know what to say," he said. "You do it. You'll think of something. Go on."

Flotsam pushed Jetsam out of the cave.

Jetsam took a few paces forward. She looked up at the seagull, gave a little cough, and called nervously, "Good morning."

The seagull didn't answer.

Jetsam tried again. "'Tis a nice day," she shouted. "Sunning good and proper. I expects you enjoys the sun, doesn't you?"

Still the seagull said nothing. It walked slowly along their roof and then sat down with its bottom in the chimney.

Jetsam's eyes widened in horror.

"It mustn't do that!" whispered Flotsam loudly. "Tell it not to, Jetsam!"

"Erm… Excuse me, Mr Gull, sir, but that there's our chimney," called Jetsam. "It would be nice if you didn't sit in it."

The seagull stared at her. It opened its beak wide and yawned. It didn't move.

"Tell it to go away!" hissed Flotsam.

Jetsam tried again. "Us was wondering if you could find another beach. Only you woke us up, see, walking up and down like that."

"Be polite!" said Flotsam helpfully.

So Jetsam added, "Please," and a little while later, "Thank you," just in case.

It was then that the bird stood up, stretched its wings and started to flap. The draught showered Jetsam with sand as the seagull took off. But it didn't fly away. It just circled the beach with lazy flaps of its vast wings. Round and round. Then it flew higher. And higher.

"'Tis leaving!" shouted Jetsam triumphantly. "Sure as knots is knots. Sure as puffins is puff—" She stopped. Her mouth dropped open.

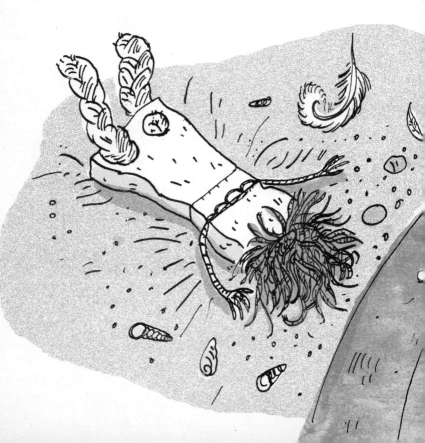

The seagull was diving straight at her!

Jetsam screamed and fell flat on her face in the sand.

The bird swooped over her head.

Then it *splatted* something on their beautiful boat house. Something wet. Something white. Something smelly.

Seagull droppings.

The bird laughed. A horrible, spiteful cackle. Then it landed on the roof and sat itself back down in the chimney.

Flotsam helped Jetsam up, and they hurried back to the safety of the cave.

"Nasty creature," said Jetsam crossly. "'Tis a terrible big bully. That's what it is. Horrid thing. Us is going to have to get rid of it. What shall us do?"

Flotsam looked at all the treasures stored in the cave. "Must be something here," he said. "Something *useful*."

They rummaged around. There were crisp packets and margarine tubs and bits of old netting and fishing floats and an old shoe.

When Flotsam reached the bottom of the first pile and had found nothing useful, he sighed and sat down. He landed on a plastic bottle, and to his surprise a jet of water shot across the cave and hit Jetsam on the foot.

"Oi!" she shouted.

Flotsam stood up.
Then he sat down
and did it again.
"Stop it!"
Jetsam cried.
But Flotsam wasn't
listening. He sat down on the floor,
cupped his bald head in his stick-like
fingers and said quietly, "I is thinking."

And after a very long time, during which
Jetsam stared hard at the seagull and the
seagull stared hard at Jetsam, Flotsam
stood up.

"I've thunk," he said.

And he began to search the cave.

Flotsam worked hard. It took nearly all day
to find just what he needed – two driftwood
planks with holes in the middle that were
lurking in the furthest, dampest, darkest
corner. When he found them, he gave a

little yell of triumph that made the seagull narrow its eyes and stare harder into the gloom of the cave.

Jetsam didn't know what Flotsam was making, but she knew that he thunk good thoughts, and so she helped. When Flotsam said, "I needs a pointy thing," Jetsam dug around until she found an old cricket stump.

"That'll do," said Flotsam. "'Tis proper perfect."

By teatime, they were ready.

"You knows what to do?" asked Flotsam.

"Oh yes," replied Jetsam, her eyes gleaming. "I knows."

With a heave and a shove they pulled Flotsam's new invention out onto the beach. The cricket stump was pushed through the holes in the planks of driftwood, holding them together in a big X. They worked like a pair of scissors. Flotsam and Jetsam

rammed the sharp end
of the cricket stump into
the sand. Before
the seagull could
take off, Flotsam and Jetsam sped back to
the cave and rolled out the
plastic bottle. They stood it
upright in the sand
pointing skywards
between two ends of the
X. Then they took up their positions.
Facing each other on opposite sides of
the X, they grasped the planks firmly.

The seagull
cackled. It soared
into the air and flew lazily
round them in big circles. It climbed higher.
Then it did just what Flotsam and Jetsam
hoped it would – it dived at them.

"NOW!" shouted Flotsam.

They raced towards each other, as fast
as their ropy little legs could carry them,
pushing the driftwood planks ahead of them.

Three things happened at
the same time.

The X shape closed with a tremendous *thwack!* and as it did, the planks squeezed the bottle hard.

Flotsam and Jetsam crashed headlong into each other and fell backwards into the sand.

And a huge fountain of smelly old sea water shot out of the bottle, soared into the air and squirted right up the bird's bottom.

The seagull squawked in surprise, did a double somersault and then crash-landed into a rock pool.

It sat there, up to its neck in water.

Flotsam and Jetsam got to their feet and brushed the sand off each other. They hugged, giggling and laughing, and clapped their hands in delight.

The bird dragged itself out of the rock pool and gave a furious flick of its wet tail feathers. With an angry screech it stretched its great wings and took off. It flew higher and higher, and this time it flew further and further away until at last it was just a speck in the distance.

"'Tis gone," said Jetsam with delight. "Us shan't see that again. Sure as soles is soles. Sure as starfish is starfish."

Flotsam and Jetsam filled the bottle with nice, fresh sea water, and then, pointing it towards their boat house, they pushed and pumped and sprayed until all the seagull droppings were washed away.

And then, feeling very happy, they sat leaning against the side of their clean house, and listened to the sea as they watched the sun sink slowly beneath the waves.

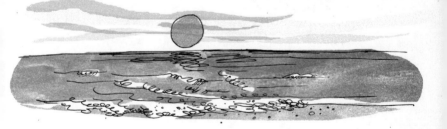

After a quiet fishing trip, the old man and the young boy left their wooden boat in the harbour and walked home along the cliff path.

If they had paused for a moment and looked down from the cliffs, they would have seen a very tidy little beach with an upturned boat in the middle that looked as if it had been washed clean. If they had looked really hard, they might have noticed an old piece of drainpipe poking out of it. And if they'd watched on a cold day, they might have seen a whisper of smoke curling out of the drainpipe, as if a cosy fire was burning inside.

But they didn't look. They didn't even glance down. To them it was just a little beach, nestling at the bottom of high cliffs: impossible to get to on foot and not worth visiting by boat – too small to bother with.

But it was the whole world to Flotsam and Jetsam.

THE BAG THAT WALKED

It was a wild and stormy night. The wind screamed at the sea, and the sea roared at the wind. Lightning crashed at the thunder, and the thunder rumbled at the lightning. It sounded to Flotsam and Jetsam as if the whole world was in a fury.

They snuggled down in their JA FA bed next to the fire, drank seaweed tea and waited for it to be over.

And in the morning, it was. The sea lay calm and still, ebbing so gently that there hardly seemed to be a tide at all. A gentle breeze stroked the surface of the water as if it was a contented cat.

It was the first warm day of spring. The air was crisp and clear, and the colours of the sea and sky and the little beach were at their brightest – as if they had been freshly painted. Sunlight flooded the boat house, pouring in through the jam-jar windows and down the chimney. It seemed to Flotsam and Jetsam as if Mother Nature herself was calling them to come outside.

"'Tis a lovely day!" cried Jetsam. "Sunning good and proper. Sure as sun is sun. Sure as blue sky is blue sky." She jumped out of the JA FA bed. "Us can paddle in the rock pools," she said eagerly.

"Us can build a sandcastle," agreed Flotsam, climbing out after her a little more slowly.

"Us can have a picnic!" cried Jetsam.

They grasped each other's hands in excitement.

But when
they stepped
outside and
looked at their
little beach, they
could see that they
were going to have a
very busy day indeed.

During the night the
sea had tossed things
up onto the sand, and
the wind had hurled
them high and wide.
There were jam jars and
yoghurt pots and shiny tin
cans. There were bits of brightly
coloured plastic and planks of wood from a
blown-down fence. There was a child's red
wellington boot, and a round orange float
that had been ripped from a fisherman's net.

A tennis ball with a hole in it had bobbed along in the waves until the sea threw it onto their little beach.

"Look!" said Flotsam in amazement. "Just look at all those treasures!"

All morning Flotsam and Jetsam carried armfuls of things across the sand. They stacked the planks and plastic in the cave. Yoghurt pots, jars and anything that might be useful for storing food were all piled neatly in one corner of their boat house. They fetched and carried and dragged and stacked until their little beach was nice and tidy once more.

They ate a picnic lunch in the warm sunshine: oarweed rolls followed by sea pink jelly and sugar kelp cream.

And then they had all afternoon to play. Flotsam built an enormous sandcastle while Jetsam paddled in the rock pools and fed the sea anemones.

When the sun started to streak the sky with pink and gold, Flotsam and Jetsam sat and watched the tide come in. Wave by wave the sea washed away Flotsam's sandcastle.

Neither of them noticed that they had left one crumpled carrier bag lying on the beach.

As the sun dipped below the horizon, turning the sea an inky black, the lone carrier bag scuttled across the beach towards Flotsam and Jetsam. It drew nearer. It stopped. It rustled at them. Flotsam and Jetsam peered at each other in the fading light. The bag rustled again.

58

"'Tis terrible strange," said Jetsam, clutching Flotsam's hand nervously.

"'Tis most peculiar," agreed Flotsam.

They sat by the boat house and watched as the bag shuffled closer.

"'Tis awful curious," murmured Jetsam.

Flotsam scratched his bald head but said nothing.

"Talk to it," said Jetsam, nudging him. "Go on. You is braver than me."

"I doesn't know what to say," Flotsam protested.

"I talked to that seagull," said Jetsam. "'Tis your turn. Think of something. Go on."

Flotsam got down on his hands and knees and crawled slowly towards the bag. "Er ... hello..." he said. "Does you want anything?"

The bag didn't answer. Flotsam extended a finger to give it a poke.

"Ow! Ow! Ow!" He leapt up and hopped around, waving his finger in the air.

"It bit me!"

"Don't be daft," said Jetsam. "'Tis a *bag*. Bags doesn't have teeth. Sure as dabs is dabs. Sure as oysters is oy—"

"Well, *you* pick it up, then," interrupted Flotsam grumpily. He retreated to the wall of the boat house and sat down crossly.

Trembling a little, Jetsam crawled towards the bag. She stretched out her hand.

"Ow! Ow! Ow!" Jetsam danced up and down, sucking her sore finger.

"Told you," said Flotsam huffily.

Jetsam ignored him. "Now look here," she said

60

sternly to the bag. "'Tisn't *right*. You can't go following folks and then biting them. 'Tisn't *polite*. 'Tisn't *nice*."

The bag rustled softly, almost as if it was saying sorry.

"That's better," said Jetsam, folding her arms across her chest.

The bag quivered nervously.

"No need to be afraid," said Jetsam kindly. "If you is going to behave, you can come inside. You must wait in the corner, nice and quiet, until us lights the fire. Then us can have a good look at you."

Inside the boat house, in the gathering dark, Flotsam lit the fire. When it was roaring away happily, he put on some featherweed stew to heat up.

Then they both turned to the bag.

"You can come here now," said Jetsam. "Over to the fire where us can see you."

The bag shuffled towards them and

stopped in front of Flotsam and Jetsam.
It trembled slightly.

"Us shan't hurt you." Jetsam scratched
her head. "I has never met a bag that could
think for itself. 'Tis terrible unnatural."

Flotsam was watching the bag carefully.
In the dim glow of the firelight he thought
he saw the glint of a beady black eye.

"I is thinking," he said quietly. "I is
thinking 'tis not just a bag. I is thinking 'tis
something in there."

The bag rustled. It was almost as if it was
nodding its head. But when Flotsam tried to
lift up the edge to see who – or what – was
inside, the bag scurried away to the darkest,
dampest corner of the boat house and
refused to come back.

Flotsam poured featherweed stew into
two jam jars and put it on the biscuit-tin
table. He put some of the lumpier bits on a
yoghurt pot lid and carried it carefully over

to the bag. He laid it gently on the floor in front of it in case whatever was inside was hungry.

Flotsam and Jetsam sat on their drinks-can chairs and ate their stew, spiking big bits of featherweed with cocktail sticks, and drinking the gravy straight from the jam jars. They watched the bag out of the corner of their eyes. After a very long time, a claw poked out of the bag, picked up a lump of stew and carried it back inside.

"I know what that is!" whispered Flotsam. "'Tis a crab in there."

"Ah," agreed Jetsam. "But what's he doing in a *bag*?"

There was a long silence while they thought about the crab.

At last Flotsam spoke again. "He's in a bag

because he's shy," he said thoughtfully. "And he's shy because he's nervous. And he's nervous because…"

"I thinks I knows!" Jetsam jumped up. "'Tis one of those hermit crabs. Those ones that wear other creatures' shells to cover their squashy behinds. I bet he lost his shell in the storm, poor thing. He's feeling all wobbly and unprotected in the rear end. No wonder he's shy. He hasn't got no clothes on!"

Two beady black eyes on two little stalks peeped out from under the bag and waggled up and down in agreement.

It was too dark to go and look for a new shell in the cave. Instead, in the light from the fire, Flotsam and Jetsam rummaged through the treasures piled in the corner of the boat house.

"'Tis a good job us keeps things here,"

said Jetsam. "Or the poor creature should have nothing to wear! Sure as cockles is cockles. Sure as scallops is scallops."

First they gave the crab a yoghurt pot. They tucked it under the edge of the bag, and turned their backs politely while he tried it on. The crab came slowly out of the bag. He walked carefully up and down in front of the fire, but the pot was too big. It fell off and the crab scuttled away with his claws clutched over his bottom. He hid in his bag, trembling with embarrassment.

They tried again. Flotsam found a tiny marmalade jar. "This'll do."

"Don't be daft," said Jetsam. "It's see-through!" She put it back and they looked again.

The little crab tried
on all sorts of things.
Fromage frais pots
(too big) and sweets tubes
(too long). Biscuit
wrappers (too noisy) and
matchboxes (too soggy).
Tin cans (too sharp) and
egg cups (too heavy).

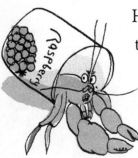

He even
tried on the tennis
ball, wriggling his tail end
through the hole before trying
to walk. But the ball rolled
suddenly backwards,
and the little crab
was carried into the
air – his legs flailing
helplessly – until
Flotsam and Jetsam
pulled him back out.

The crab tried on everything that was stacked in the corner. And just when they were thinking that the poor creature would have to live in his plastic bag for ever, Jetsam had an idea.

"I has had a thunk!" she cried.

Jetsam pulled aside the blanket of their JA FA bed and scrabbled down into the dried seaweed beneath. In the corner, right at the very bottom, was their most precious treasure. It was very small and very shiny: a silver thimble which had rolled from the deck of an ocean liner a long time ago. The sea had laid it gently down on the beach for Flotsam and Jetsam.

And now Jetsam carried it over and tucked it under the bag.

There was a hushed silence. The bag quivered with excitement. Then – with a swish and a flick – the crab threw aside his carrier bag and paraded up and down in front of the fire. He marched, he twirled, he strutted, he pranced. He looked magnificent. And as he wiggled the thimble from side to side, it seemed as if he was wagging his tail.

Flotsam and Jetsam squeezed together onto the football armchair and watched. When he had finished showing off (which took until nearly midnight), the crab curled up on the floor at their feet and fell asleep.

"Us can't leave him by the fire," whispered Jetsam. "Poor little chap will dry out. Sure as salt is salt. Sure as heat is heat." She nudged Flotsam. "Go and sort him a bed. That red thing will do. Go on. I is scared of the dark."

Flotsam went out into the night, pulling the wellington boot behind him. He filled the foot with sand, topped it up with sea water and dragged it back inside. Jetsam helped him wedge it into the coldest, dampest corner of the boat house, where the crab would be most comfortable.

Then – very gently so as not to wake him – they picked him up, dropped him into the boot and tucked him in with a piece of seaweed.

Flotsam and Jetsam stood watching him sleep. A stream of tiny bubbles rose from the thimble.

"Nice little chap, isn't he?" said Flotsam softly.

"He is that."

There was a long pause.

"Can us keep him?" asked Flotsam.

"'Twould be terrible nice," agreed Jetsam. "Shall us give him a name?"

"That bag had something written on it."

They smoothed out the crumpled carrier bag and sighed happily.

"Sainsbury," they said with satisfaction.

Every day, the old man and the young boy walked over the cliffs and down to the harbour where their wooden fishing boat bobbed eagerly in the water.

If they had paused for a moment and looked down from the cliffs, they would have seen a very tidy little beach with an upturned boat in the middle. If they had looked really hard, they might have noticed a thin line in the sand – about as wide as the heel of a child's wellington boot – where something had been dragged from the edge of the sea into the boat through a crack in the side.

But they didn't look. They didn't even glance down. To them it was just a little beach, nestling at the bottom of high cliffs: impossible to get to on foot and not worth visiting by boat – too small to bother with.

But it was the whole world to Flotsam and Jetsam.

THE BEACH
BALL

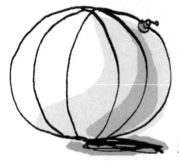

It rained all night.

Flotsam and Jetsam
didn't mind the rain.

Not if they were tucked
up, nice and dry, in their JA FA bed by the
fire in the boat house. In the worst winter
storms they would huddle down under their
blanket, holding hands tightly. From the
warmth and safety of their bed they would
listen to the muffled screams of the wind
and the crashing of the sea as it hurled itself
angrily against the cliffs.

But on this particular night something

happened. Just when the rain was at its rainiest and the dark was at its darkest, Jetsam heard something.

Plop!

For a minute, she thought the seagull had come back and was doing something it shouldn't down the chimney.

"Go away, you nasty great bully!" she shouted.

Plop!

Then she wondered if Sainsbury had fallen out of his wellington boot.

"Are you all right, Sainsbury?" she called.

Plop!

Then she realized that her head was wet.

Plop!

She looked up at the roof.

Plop!

A drop of rainwater landed in her eye.

"Flotsam!" She shook him awake.

He yawned. "Whassamadder?"

"Us is leaking."

Plop!

"Sure as water is water."

Plop!

"Sure as big plopping dollops is big plopping dollops."

Plop!

Flotsam sat up and groaned. "I is thinking," he mumbled, rubbing his eyes. There was a long pause. "I thunk us can't do much about it now." He sighed sleepily. "'Tis too dark. Us will just have to move to a dry spot."

Climbing reluctantly out of the warm JA FA bed, they heaved and prodded and shoved it until at last they had pushed it away from the leak.

Then they climbed back in, pulled the blanket over their heads and went back to sleep.

Plop! Plop! Plop!

Crash!

Sperlosh!

"AAAARRRGGGHHHH!"

A very large, very wet slab of roof had landed on them, bruising their toeless feet and giving them a terrible fright. The rain poured in. Flotsam and Jetsam were drenched.

Flotsam and Jetsam spent the rest of the night huddled under the sodden blanket at one end of the boat house.

Sainsbury had been woken up by Flotsam and Jetsam's shouting, followed by their grumbling. He took himself off to the other end. He didn't mind the wet, but he didn't like it when Flotsam and Jetsam were cross. Sainsbury climbed into the JA FA bed, and slept happily in the shower of rainwater.

By the morning, the rain had stopped, but Flotsam and Jetsam were cold and hungry and very, very grumpy. They looked up at the large hole in the roof. Their cosy boat house was ruined.

"What shall us do?" demanded Jetsam.

"Us hasn't got nothing to mend it with,"

grumbled Flotsam. "And I is too cold to have a good thunk."

"Us shall just have to move back into the cave," said Jetsam crossly.

"Ah," agreed Flotsam. "Us shall."

The thought of going back to live in the damp, dark, smoky cave didn't improve their tempers. They scowled at each other as they stoked the fire. They frowned at each other as they made the tea. They growled at each other as they fetched the breakfast things.

Sainsbury sat in the wet bed and trembled nervously.

Flotsam thumped limpet shells of tea down into the dents on the biscuit-tin table. Jetsam slammed the tub of bladderwrack crispies in between them, making the shells wobble and spilling hot tea.

With a sulky grunt, Jetsam sat down on her drinks-can chair and grabbed a handful of crispies. She crammed some into her mouth, chewed once, and then spat them out in disgust.

"These is not bladderwrack *crispies*!" she shrieked. "These is bladderwrack *soggies*!"

It was true. They had been dripped on in the night and didn't taste very nice.

"'Tis all us have got," growled Flotsam, filling his mouth with soggies. He chewed with great determination and forced himself to swallow. Then he shuddered from head to foot. He didn't eat any more.

Tired, cold, grumpy and now hungry too, Flotsam and Jetsam got ready for their move back to the cave. They pulled on their waterproof Walkers.

Flotsam whistled for Sainsbury. "'Tis time for your paddle."

Sainsbury scuttled gratefully to the door.

But he couldn't get out. Something very large and very pink was blocking the entrance.

It was a beach ball. The sea had carried it from another beach. During the night the wind had blown it up to the boat house and wedged it tightly in the doorway with a particularly savage gust. Flotsam tried pushing against it. It was soft and squeaky and slippery.

It didn't move.

"Now what?" said Jetsam crossly. She stared at the ball furiously. If it had been alive it would have run away with its tail between its legs. But it was plastic, so it stayed where it was.

With a thunderous scream of "Boiling bladderwrack!" Jetsam ran at it. She sank into the soft yielding plastic for a second. Then she bounced backwards and landed on the football armchair.

Jetsam sat blinking in surprise. She thought for a moment. Then she stood up, and did it again.

Jetsam ran full pelt at the
beach ball. She gave a small
jump and flung herself headlong
at the pink plastic. She hit it about
halfway up and rebounded across
the boat house.

The beach ball didn't move,
but Jetsam started giggling.

"'Tis terrible funny," she told Flotsam
when she had got her breath back. "'Tis
marvellous amusing. You has a go. Go on."

Flotsam ran at the pink plastic ball.

Boing!

He bounced off it and landed on the
football armchair. He stood up and laughed
until tears ran down his pebble-smooth
cheeks.

Then he stopped laughing and said,
"I is thinking." He paused for a moment,
scratching his head, and looked at the
football armchair thoughtfully. "I've thunk."

He dragged the
armchair across the floor
and placed it a little way
from the beach ball.

Flotsam took a few paces
back. He narrowed his eyes,
judging the distance. Then
he ran, gave a little jump onto
the football armchair and
trampolined off it onto
the beach ball.

BOING!!!

He flew right across the boat
house and landed in the soggy JA FA bed.

Then it was Jetsam's turn. She
sprinted, bounced on the armchair,
hit the beach ball and
turned a perfect somersault
before landing beside Flotsam.

They each had
another turn.

"'Tis wonderful!" said Jetsam. "'Tis marvellous funny. 'Tis cheered me up good and proper."

A faint squeal from the floor attracted her attention. Sainsbury was staring up at them with pleading eyes.

"Sorry, Sainsbury," Jetsam said. "You is right. 'Tis *your* turn. Sure as plaice is plaice. Sure as guillemots is guillemots."

Sainsbury was excited. He wiggled his thimble. He extended his legs. He bounced up and down on the spot like a runner getting ready for a big race. Then he scuttled as fast as his little legs would carry him. With an almighty leap, he threw

himself onto the armchair
and somersaulted across to
the beach ball. Flotsam
and Jetsam waited
for him to
bounce back
and fly
through the air
onto the bed.

But he didn't.

There was a hushed silence.

Flotsam and Jetsam looked at
the beach ball.

Sainsbury was stuck near the top. One of
his claws had pierced the plastic. He hung
there, his beady black eyes blinking
nervously.

"Poor little Sainsbury," said Flotsam. "Don't worry. Us'll get you down."

Flotsam and Jetsam dragged their drinks-can chairs over to the beach ball and stood on them. It was a little wobbly, but they grabbed hold of Sainsbury and they heaved and they tugged and finally there was a *pop!* They all crashed to the floor in an untidy heap, but Sainsbury was free.

Then Jetsam said in a scared little whisper, "Can you hear that? 'Tis a terrible whooshing! A horrible hooshing! What's happening?"

Before their eyes the beach ball got smaller and smaller and flatter and flatter

until it lay in the door like a wrinkled pink
plastic mat.

A little tear oozed from Sainsbury's eye
and plopped onto his claw.

"Oh, poor Sainsbury," said Jetsam, patting
him sadly. "'Tis a terrible pity. Oh, 'tis a
terrible shame. Sure as whales is whales.
Sure as turtles is turtles."

"'Tis that," agreed Flotsam. "Poor little
fellow."

There was a long pause.

Suddenly Jetsam picked up the limp piece
of pink plastic and stared at it. "I has had a
thunk!" she cried. "Us shan't need to move
back to that nasty smoky old cave after all!
I knows how to mend the roof!"

To cheer Sainsbury up, Flotsam and Jetsam dragged the football armchair back across the floor. Sainsbury scuttled across the boat house, threw himself onto the armchair and bounced in an elegant curve onto the JA FA bed. Then he raced back and did it again.

While Sainsbury played, Flotsam and Jetsam patched the roof, hammering the beach ball down with some rusty nails and a large pebble. Later they made a delicious lunch of seaweed sausages and milkwort mash.

After they'd eaten lunch, Flotsam and
Jetsam dragged the JA FA bed outside to dry
in the afternoon sun. Sainsbury was staring
at the football armchair with his beady black
eyes.

"What does you want, Sainsbury?" asked
Jetsam. "Has *you* been thinking a thunk too?
Does you want us to do something?"

Sainsbury waggled his thimble.

"Does you want us to take it outside?"

Sainsbury bounced up and down.

"Does you want to play with it on the
beach?"

Sainsbury scuttled round and round in
excited circles.

Flotsam and Jetsam dragged the football
armchair onto the beach. Sainsbury wiggled
his thimble and extended his legs. He
bounced up and down on the spot like a
runner getting ready for a big race. Then,
with a squeal of excitement, he scuttled as

fast as his little legs could carry him across
the beach. With an almighty leap, he threw
himself onto the armchair. There was a loud
BOING! and Sainsbury performed
a magnificent triple
somersault into the
nearest rock pool.

Splash!
Flotsam and Jetsam gasped.
"'Tis amazing!"
"'Tis proper wonderful!"
They clapped and cheered.
Sainsbury kept it up all afternoon. He
dived, he somersaulted, he did half-twists
and backflips until, when the sun started to

set, he curled up on the sand beside Flotsam and Jetsam and yawned a very big yawn.

"Lovely little Sainsbury," said Jetsam, patting his claw fondly. "Who'd have thunk you was such a clever crab!"

And then, feeling very happy, they all sat leaning against the side of their boat house, and listened to the sea as they watched the sun sink slowly beneath the waves.

After a quiet day's
fishing, the old man and
the young boy walked
home along the cliff path. If
they had paused for a moment and
looked down from the cliffs, they would
have seen a very tidy little beach with an
upturned boat in the middle. If they had looked
really hard, they might have noticed a flash of
pink where someone had mended a leak. And
if they'd watched on a cold day, they might
have seen a whisper of smoke curling out of the
drainpipe, as if a cosy fire was
burning inside.

But they didn't look. They didn't even glance down. To them it was just a little beach, nestling at the bottom of high cliffs: impossible to get to on foot and not worth visiting by boat – too small to bother with.

Nobody has ever stopped. Nobody has ever looked down. The beach remains unnoticed and undisturbed, which is just as well.

It is the whole world to Flotsam and Jetsam …and Sainsbury.

TANYA LANDMAN studied for a degree in English literature at Liverpool University, before working in a bookshop, an arts centre, and a zoo. Since 1992, Tanya has been part of Storybox Theatre, working as a writer, administrator and performer – a job which has taken her to festivals all over the world. She is the author of *Waking Merlin*, a novel for young readers, and its sequel, *Merlin's Apprentice* (published October 2006). She lives with her family in Devon.

RUTH RIVERS was brought up in the East Midlands and now lives in London. She almost dropped art aged fourteen as she wanted to be a vet – but luckily she was persuaded to continue and went on to study Graphic Design at Exeter College of Art and Design. She spent a number of years working in advertising before going on to illustrate children's books, which include *The Biggest Bible Storybook* by Anne Adeney and *Matty Mouse* by Jenny Nimmo.